The Sparkplugs Move In

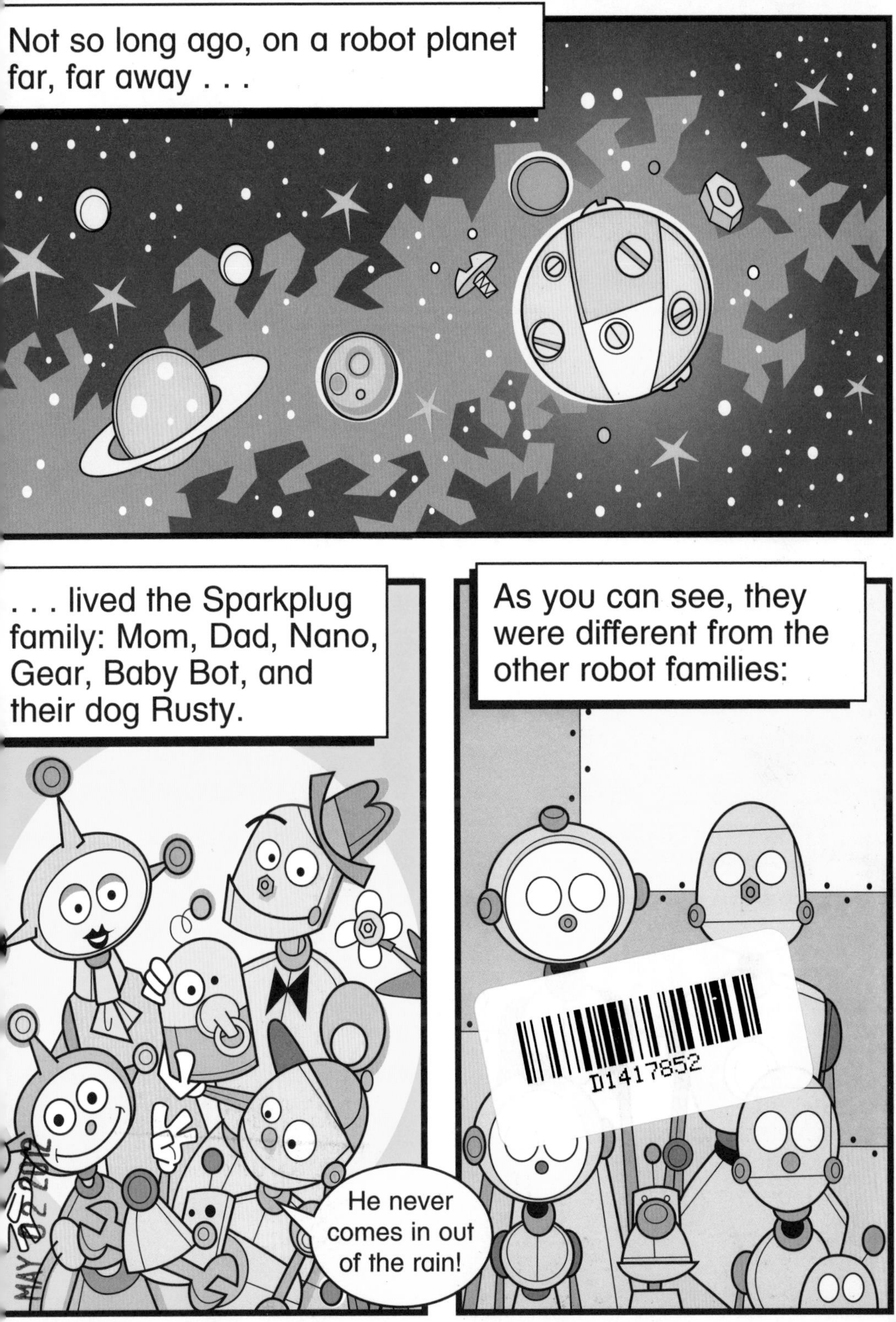
Not so long ago, on a robot planet far, far away . . .
. . . lived the Sparkplug family: Mom, Dad, Nano, Gear, Baby Bot, and their dog Rusty.
He never comes in out of the rain!
As you can see, they were different from the other robot families:

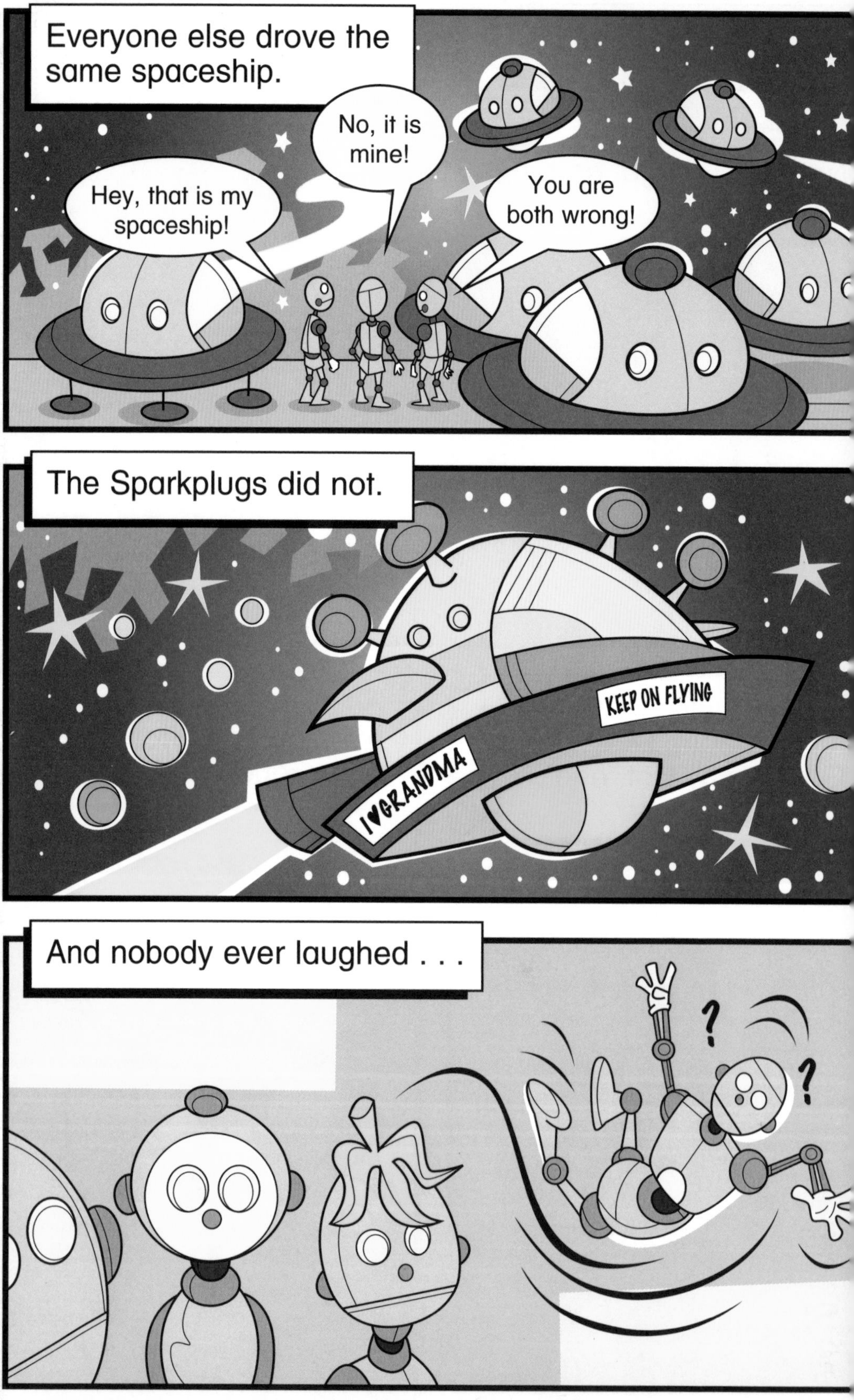

Everyone else drove the same spaceship.
Hey, that is my spaceship!
No, it is mine!
You are both wrong!
The Sparkplugs did not.
KEEP ON FLYING
I ♥ GRANDMA
And nobody ever laughed . . .
?
?

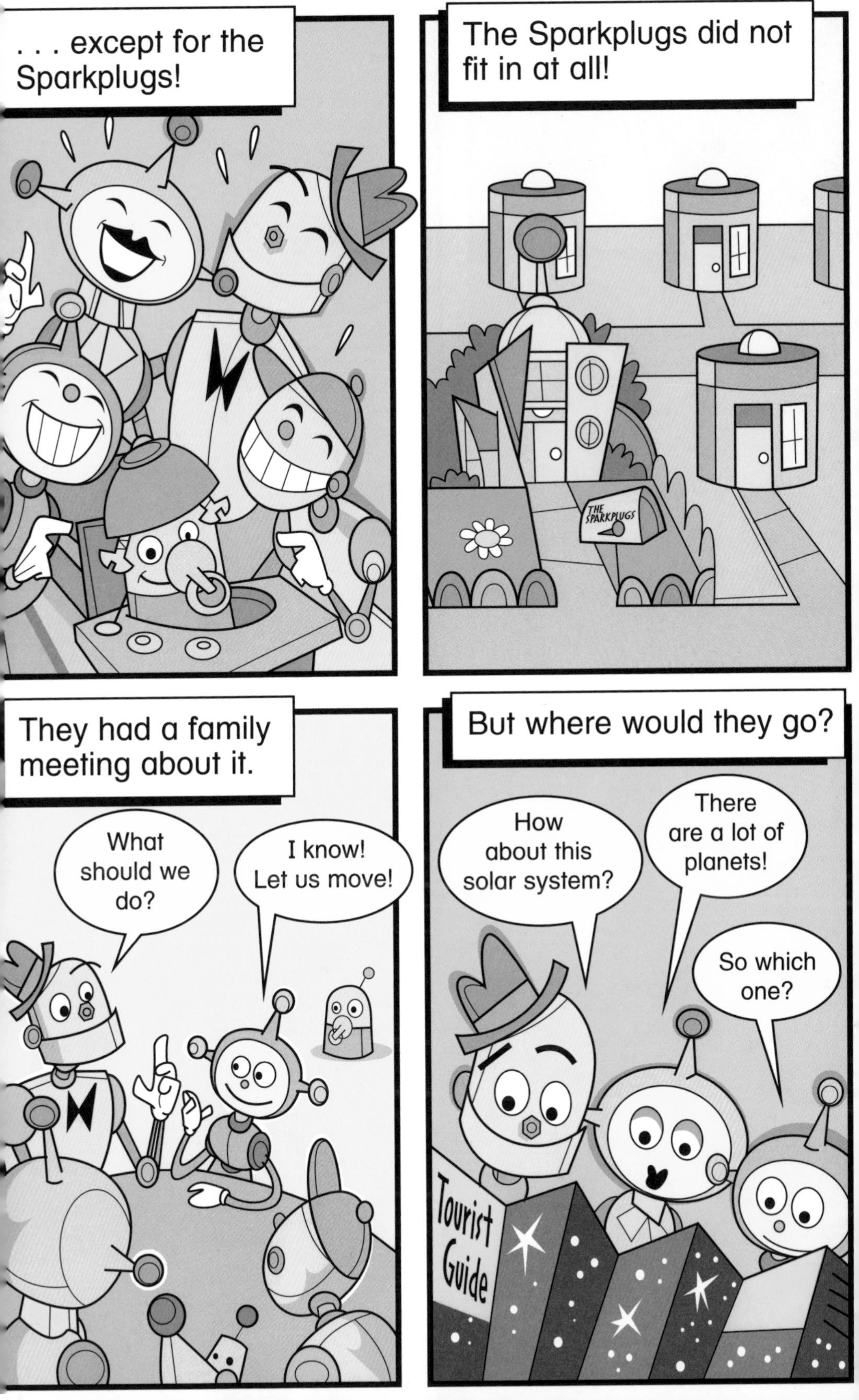
. . . except for the Sparkplugs!
The Sparkplugs did not fit in at all!
THE SPARKPLUGS
They had a family meeting about it.
What should we do?
I know! Let us move!
But where would they go?
How about this solar system?
There are a lot of planets!
So which one?
Tourist Guide

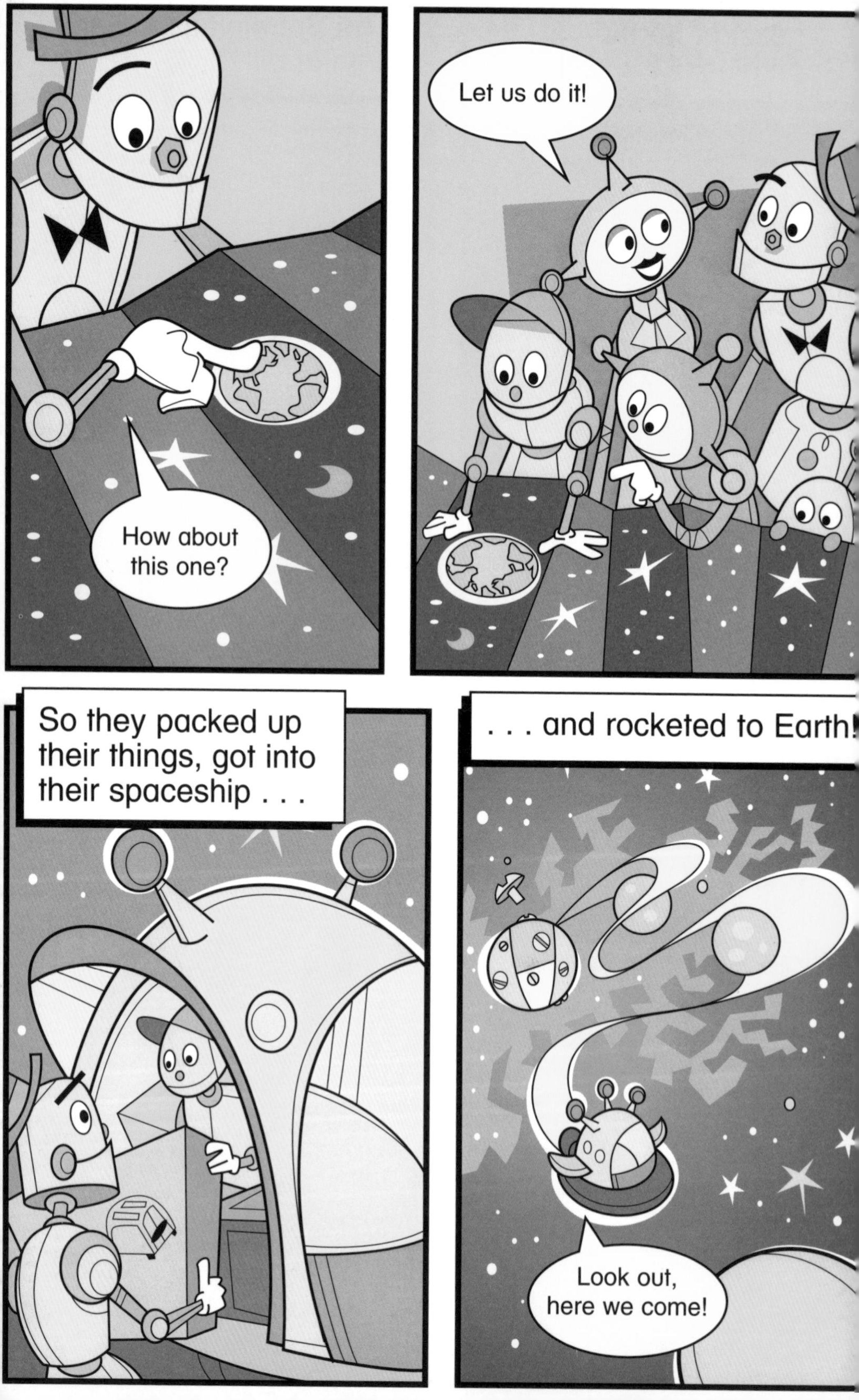
How about this one?
Let us do it!
So they packed up their things, got into their spaceship . . .
. . . and rocketed to Earth!
Look out, here we come!

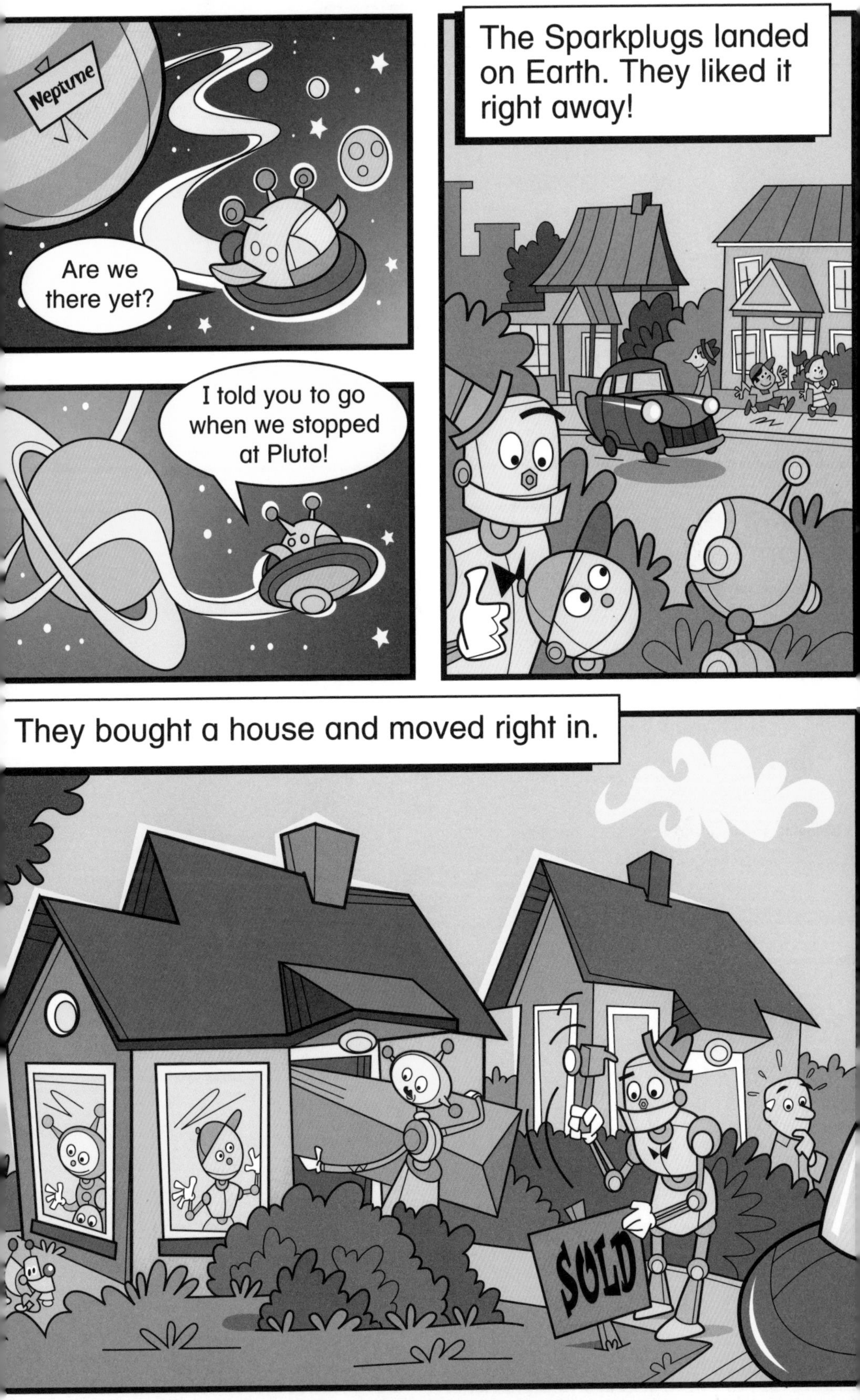
Neptune
Are we there yet?
I told you to go when we stopped at Pluto!
The Sparkplugs landed on Earth. They liked it right away!
They bought a house and moved right in.
SOLD

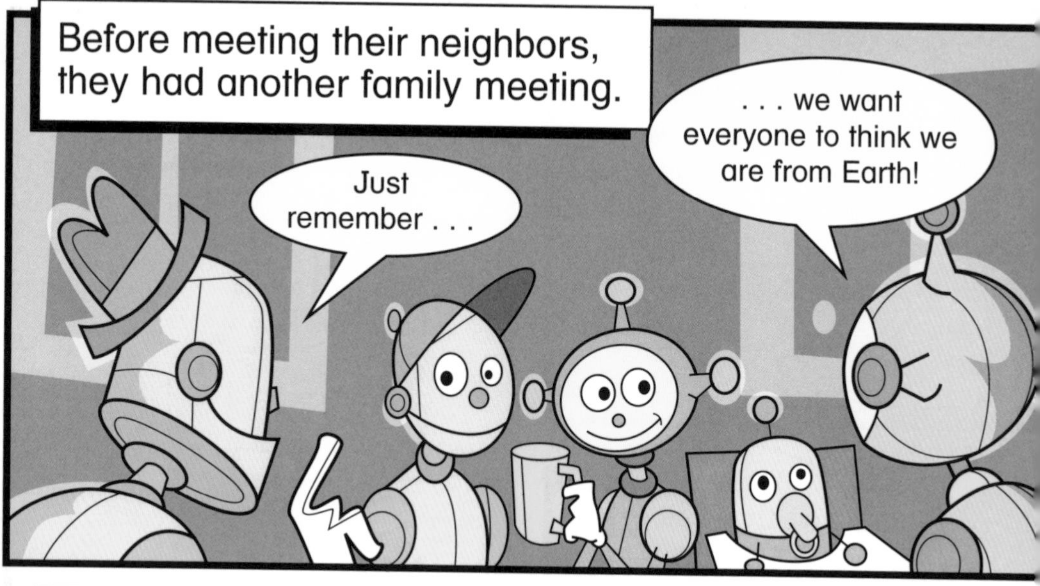
Before meeting their neighbors, they had another family meeting.
Just remember . . .
. . . we want everyone to think we are from Earth!

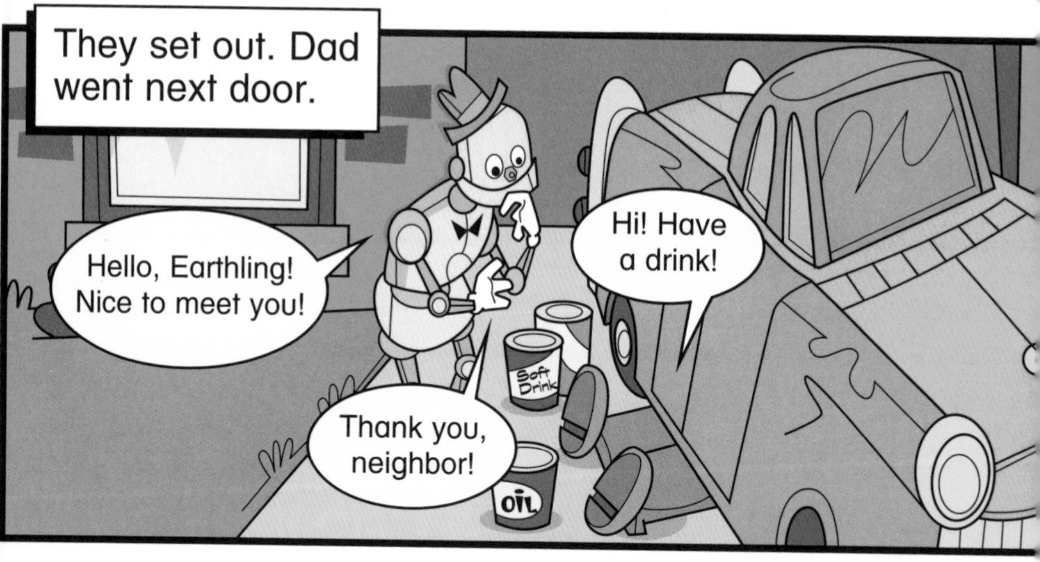
They set out. Dad went next door.
Hi! Have a drink!
Hello, Earthling! Nice to meet you!
Thank you, neighbor!
Soft Drink
OIL

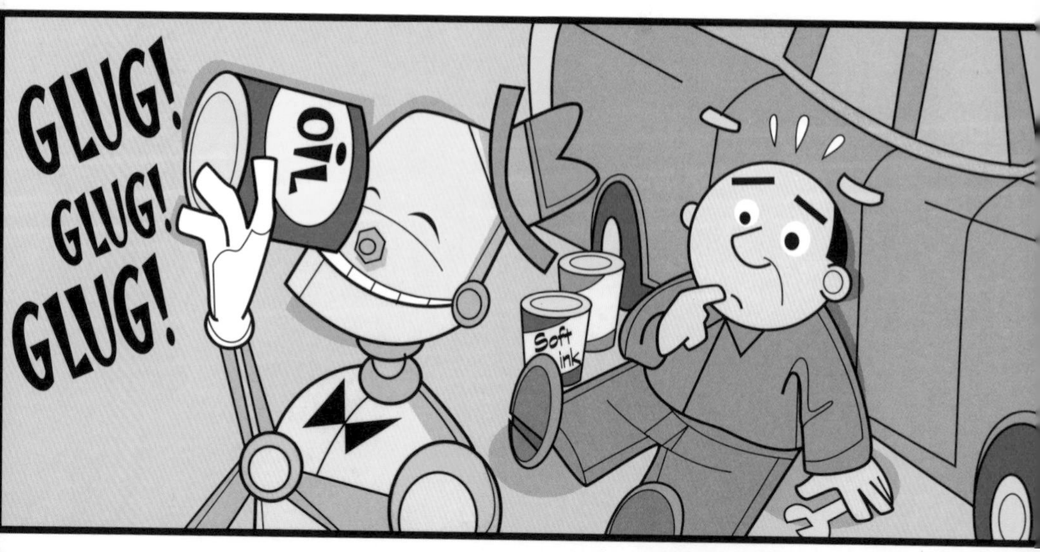
GLUG!
GLUG!
GLUG!
OIL

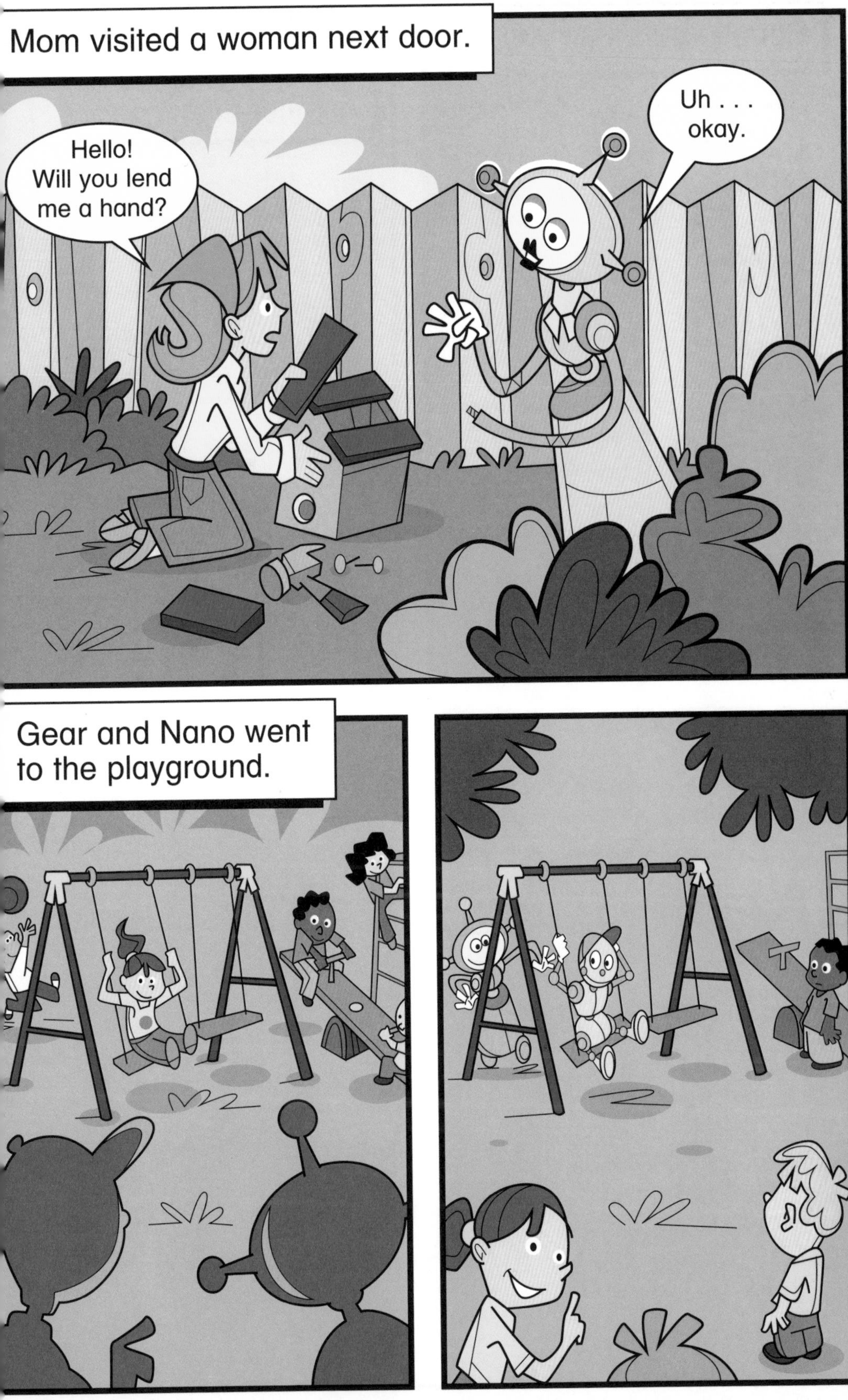
Mom visited a woman next door.
Hello! Will you lend me a hand?
Uh . . . okay.
Gear and Nano went to the playground.

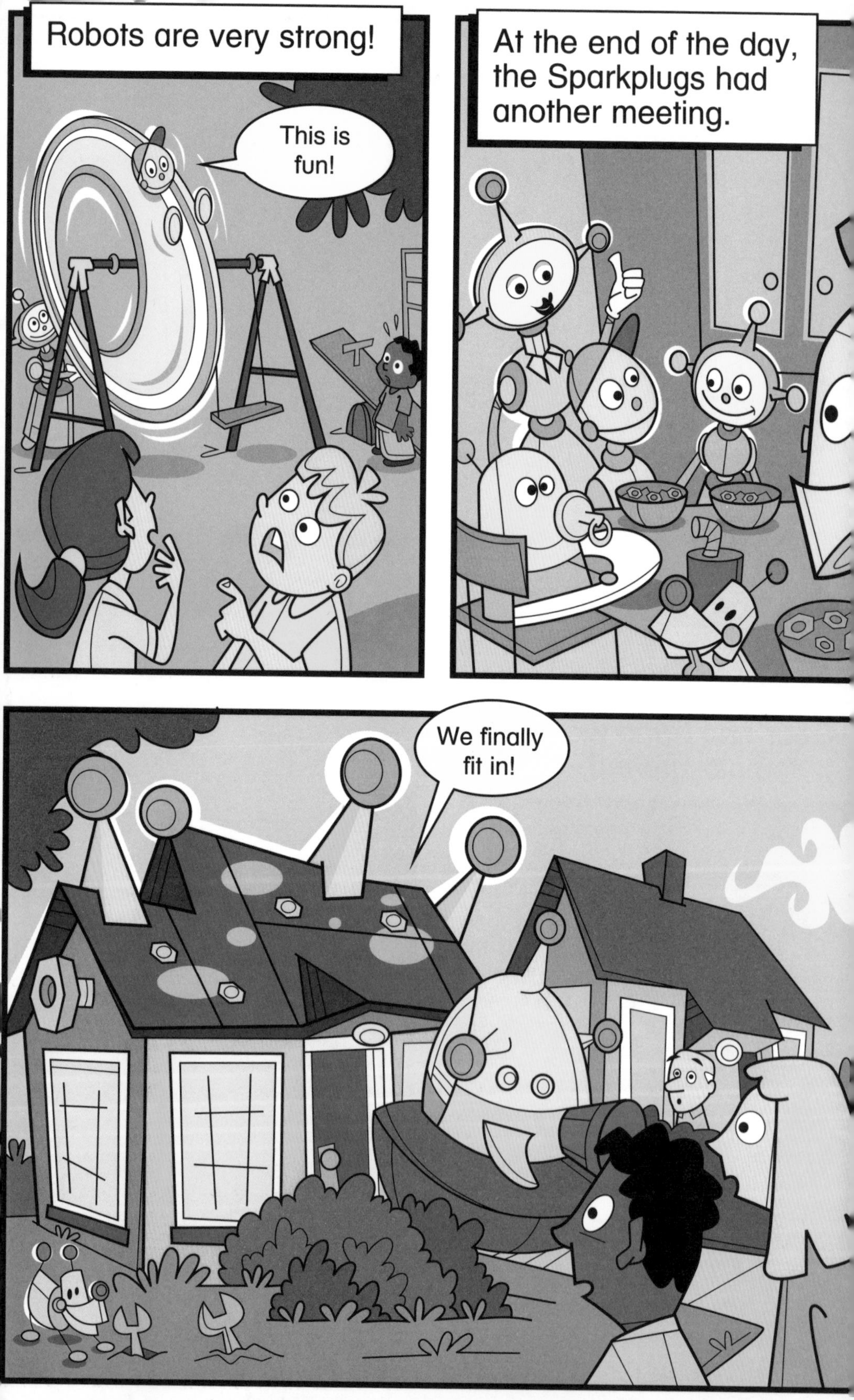
Robots are very strong!
This is fun!
At the end of the day, the Sparkplugs had another meeting.
We finally fit in!

School Daze

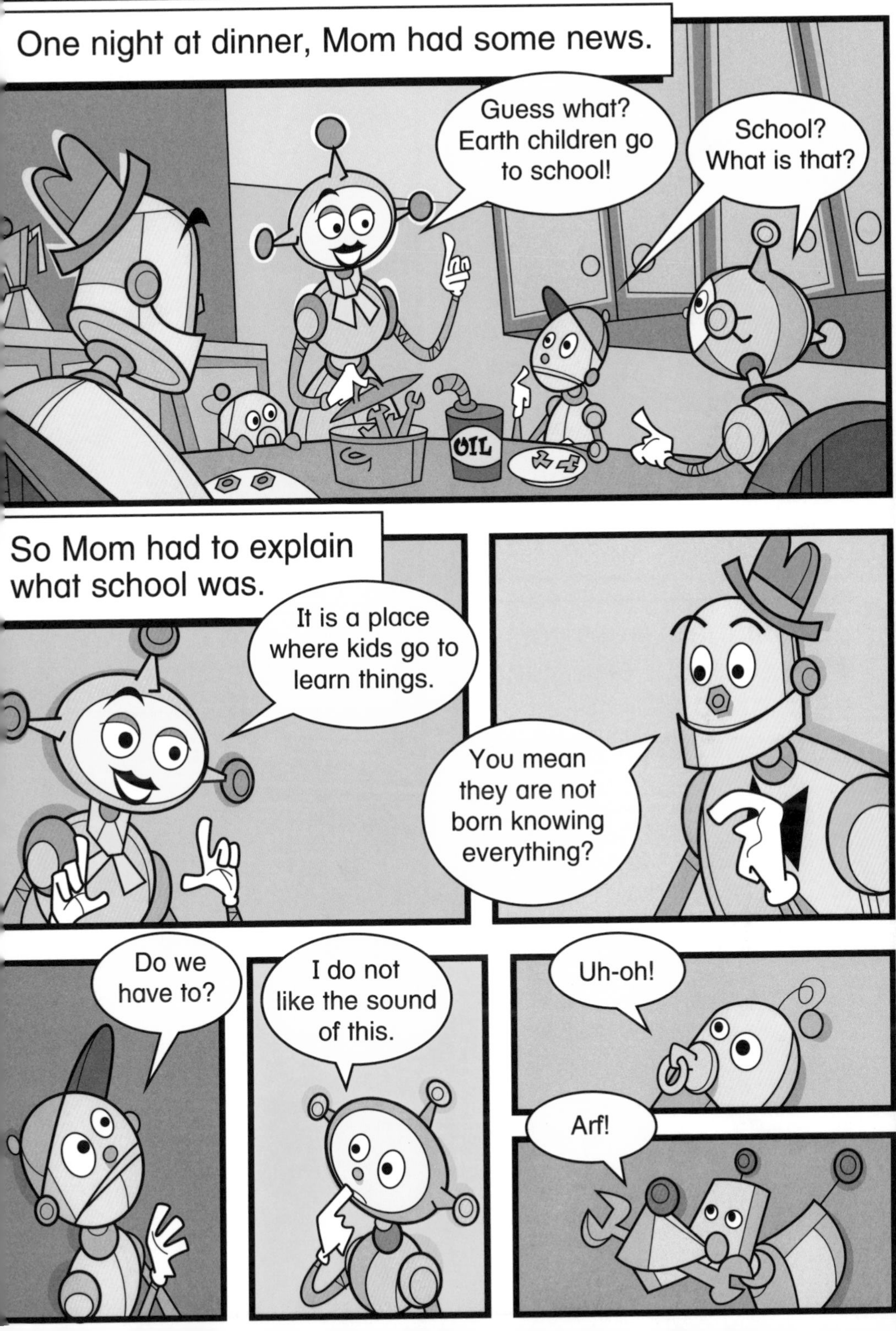
One night at dinner, Mom had some news.
Guess what? Earth children go to school!
School? What is that?
So Mom had to explain what school was.
It is a place where kids go to learn things.
You mean they are not born knowing everything?
Do we have to?
I do not like the sound of this.
Uh-oh!
Arf!
OIL

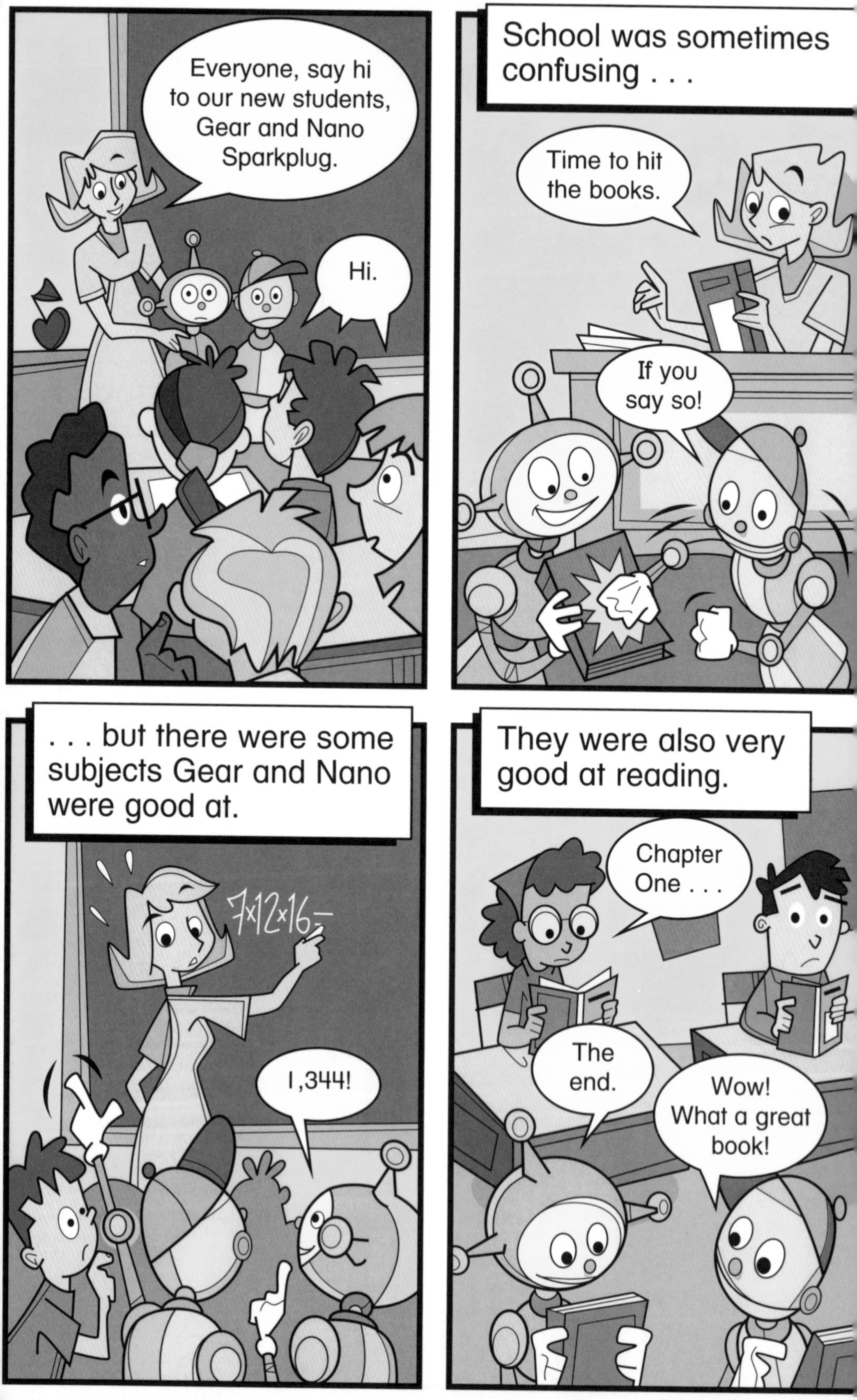
Everyone, say hi to our new students, Gear and Nano Sparkplug.
Hi.
School was sometimes confusing . . .
Time to hit the books.
If you say so!
. . . but there were some subjects Gear and Nano were good at.
7×12×16=
1,344!
They were also very good at reading.
Chapter One . . .
The end.
Wow! What a great book!

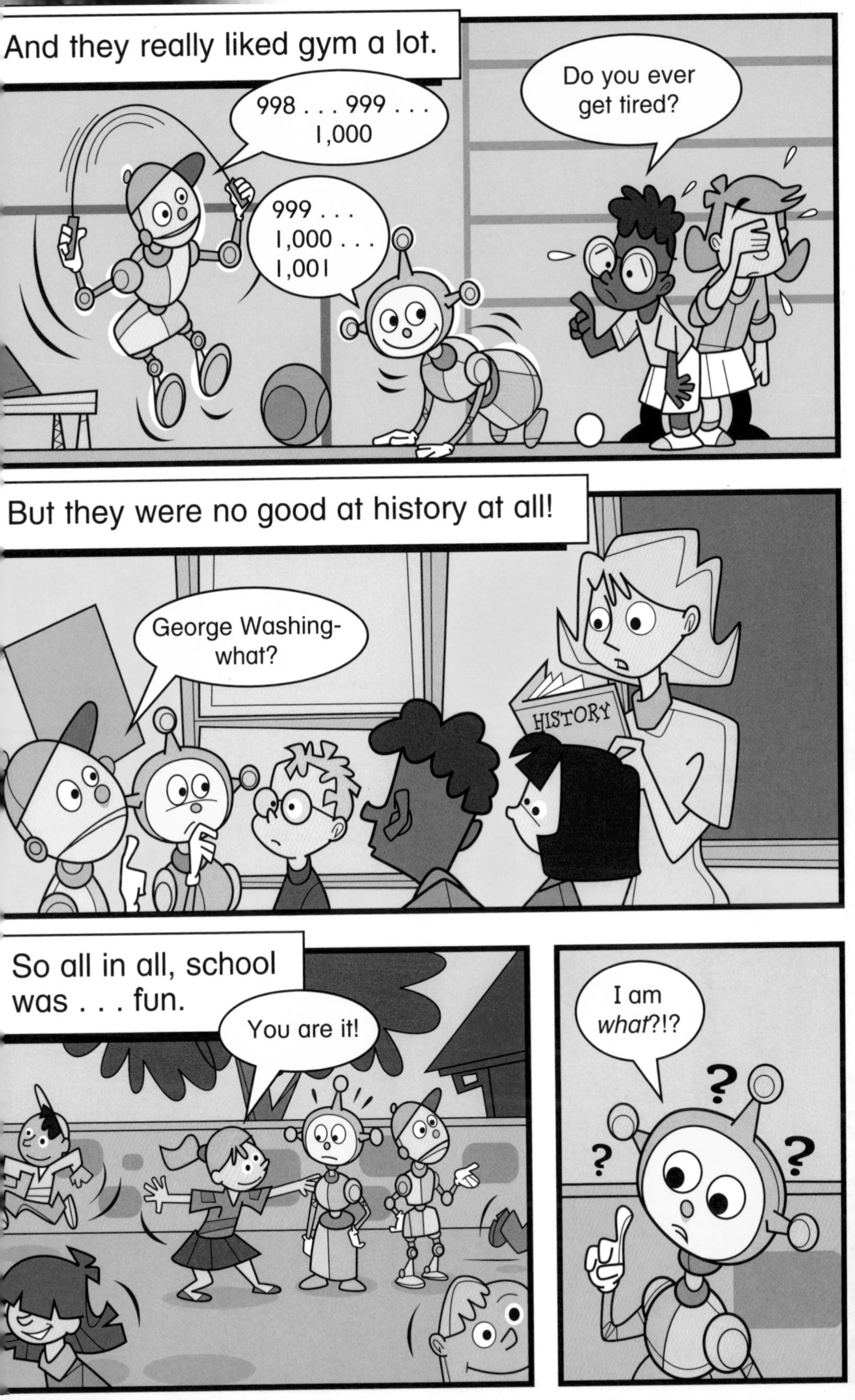
And they really liked gym a lot.
998 . . . 999 . . . 1,000
999 . . . 1,000 . . . 1,001
Do you ever get tired?
But they were no good at history at all!
George Washing-what?
HISTORY
So all in all, school was . . . fun.
You are it!
I am *what*?!?

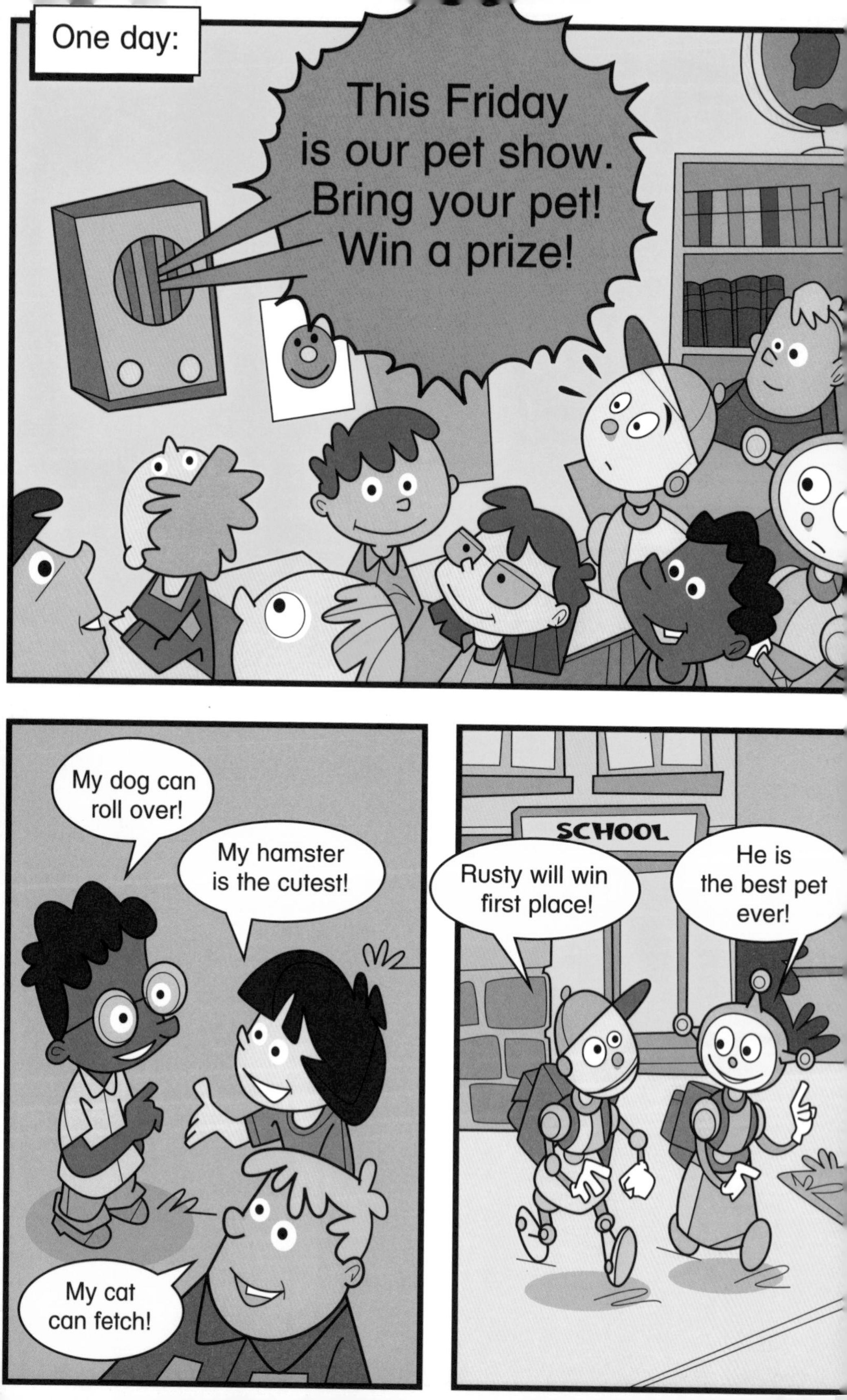

One day:
This Friday is our pet show. Bring your pet! Win a prize!
My dog can roll over!
My hamster is the cutest!
My cat can fetch!
SCHOOL
Rusty will win first place!
He is the best pet ever!

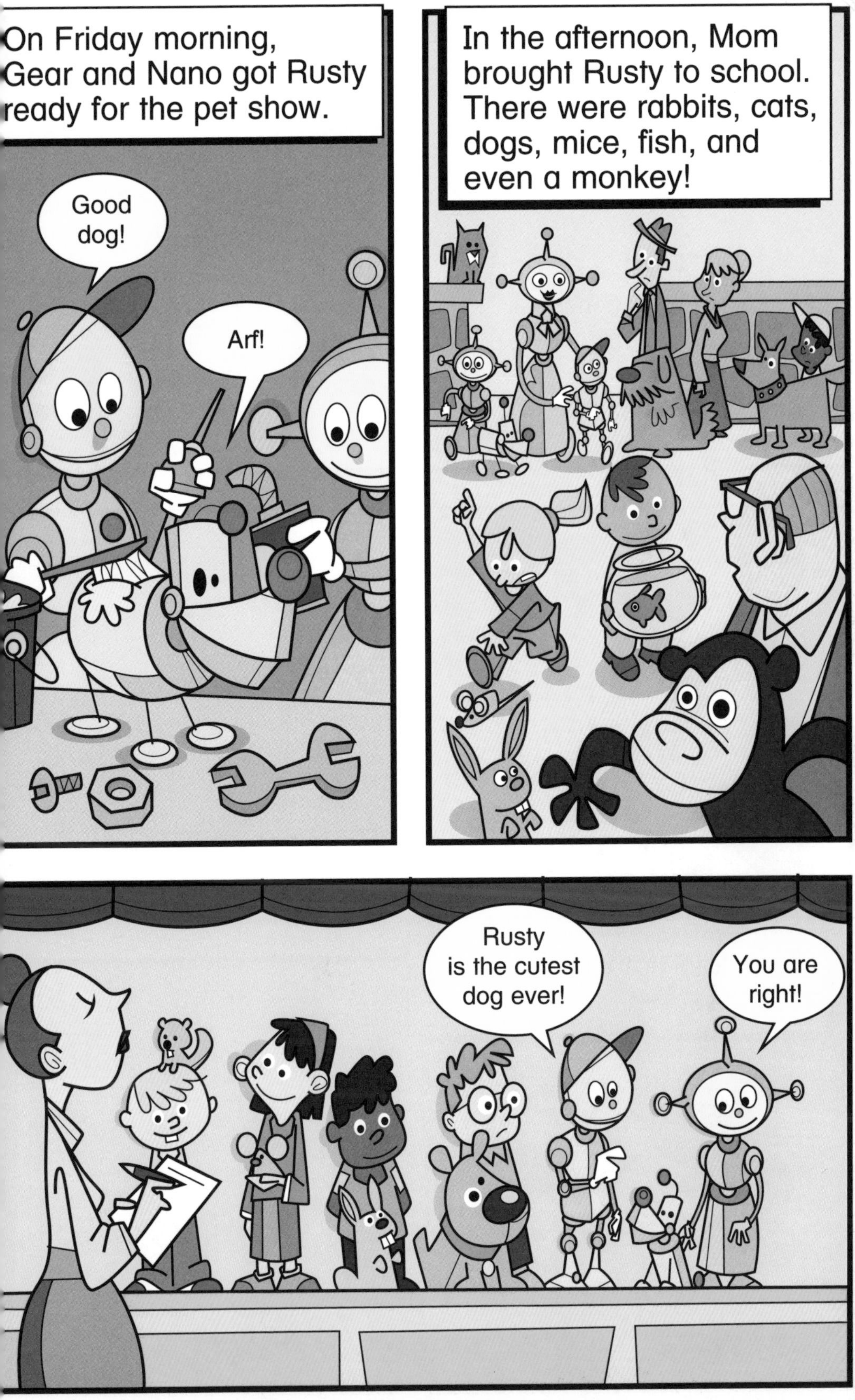
On Friday morning, Gear and Nano got Rusty ready for the pet show.
Good dog!
Arf!
In the afternoon, Mom brought Rusty to school. There were rabbits, cats, dogs, mice, fish, and even a monkey!
Rusty is the cutest dog ever!
You are right!

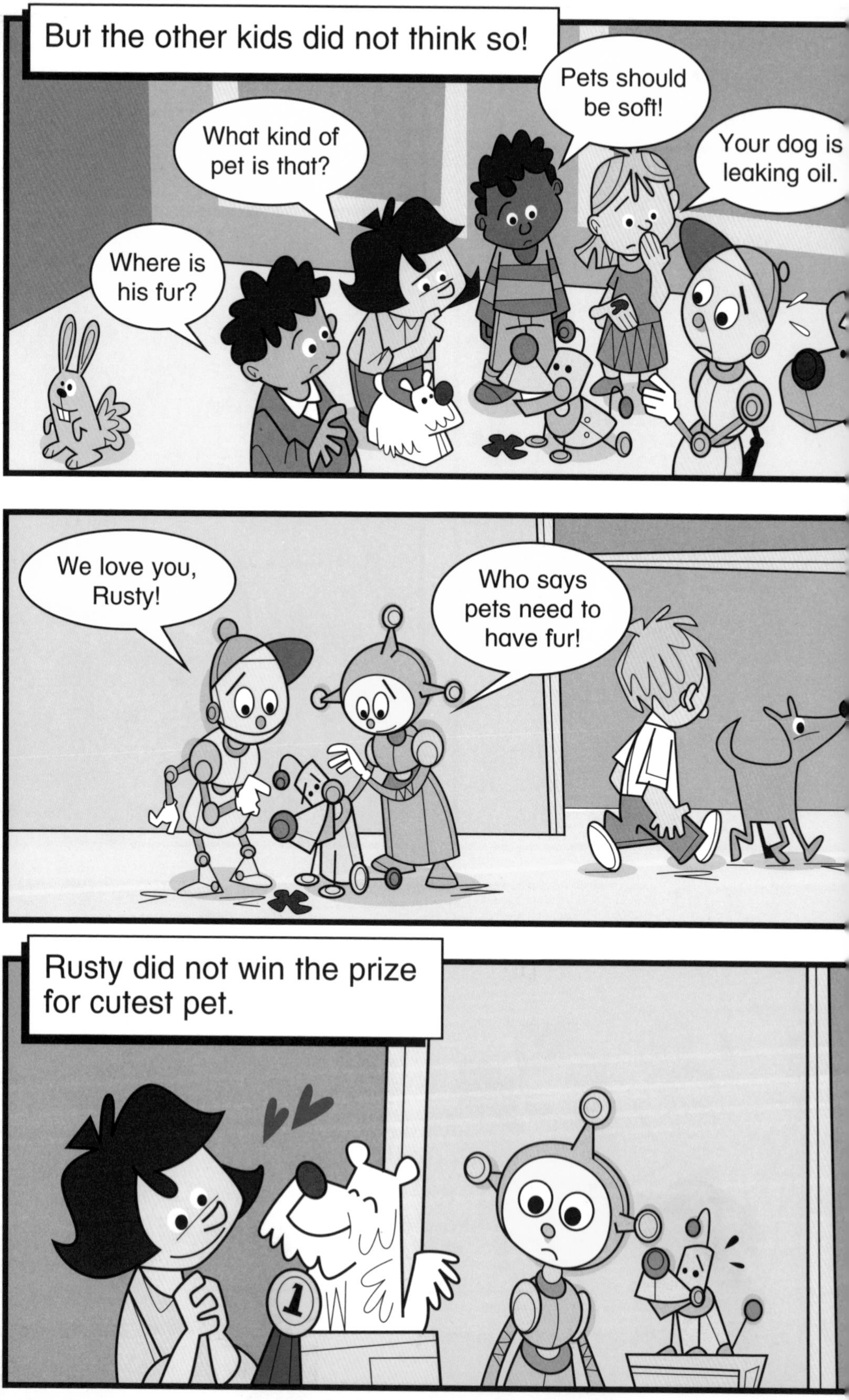
But the other kids did not think so!
Where is his fur?
What kind of pet is that?
Pets should be soft!
Your dog is leaking oil.
We love you, Rusty!
Who says pets need to have fur!
Rusty did not win the prize for cutest pet.

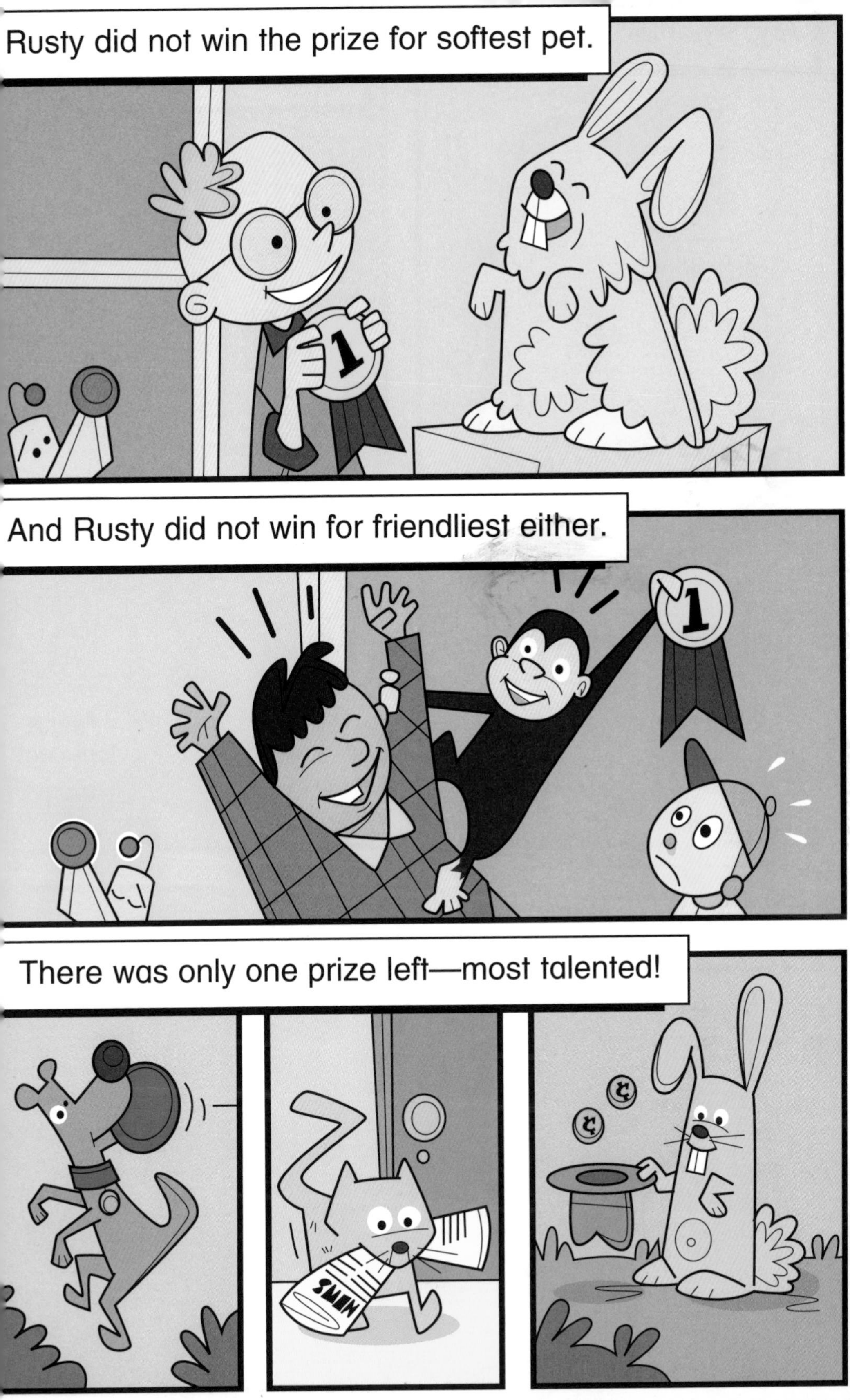
Rusty did not win the prize for softest pet.
And Rusty did not win for friendliest either.
There was only one prize left—most talented!

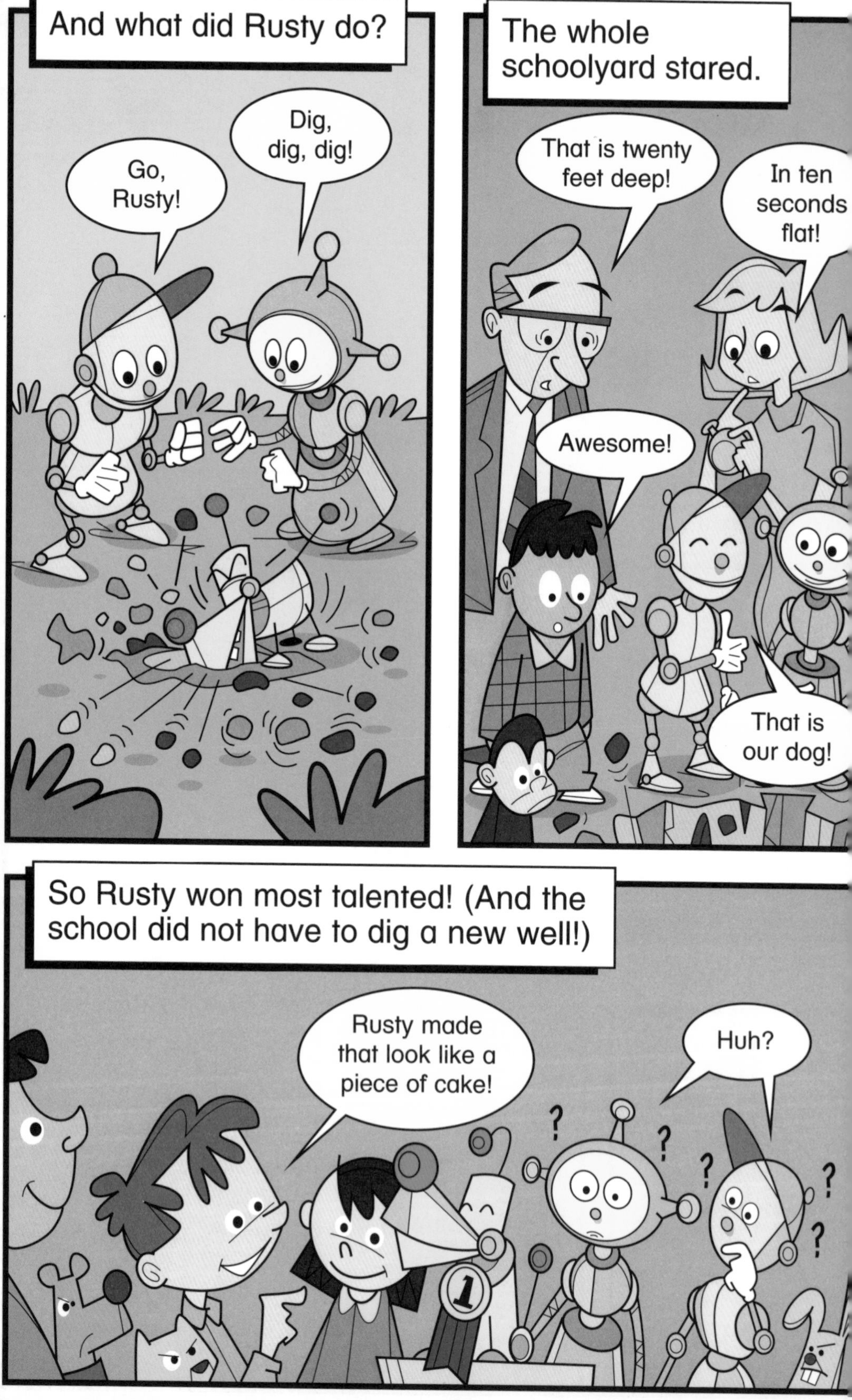
And what did Rusty do?
Go, Rusty!
Dig, dig, dig!
The whole schoolyard stared.
That is twenty feet deep!
In ten seconds flat!
Awesome!
That is our dog!
So Rusty won most talented! (And the school did not have to dig a new well!)
Rusty made that look like a piece of cake!
Huh?

The Sparkplugs' first Halloween!

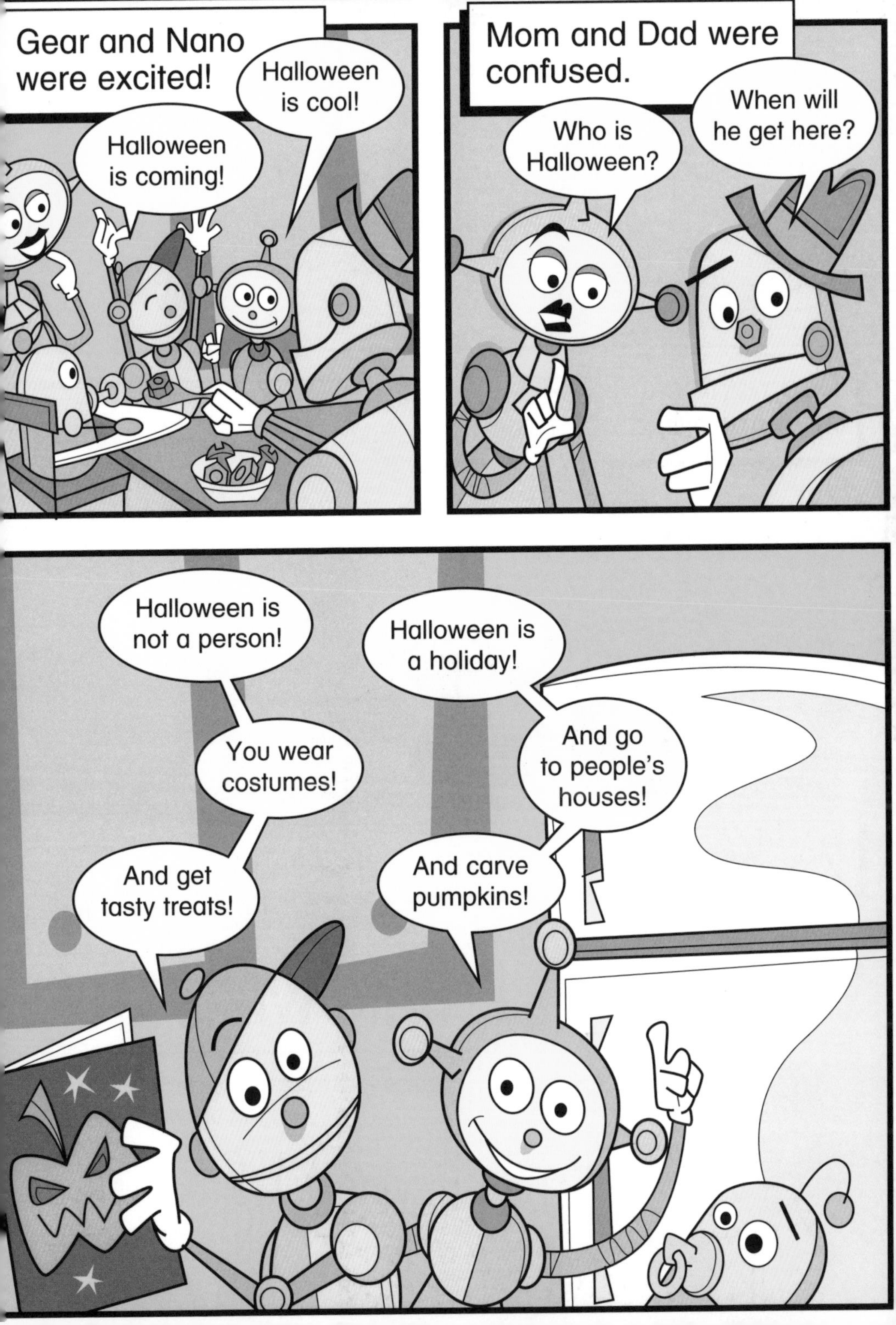
Gear and Nano were excited!
Halloween is coming!
Halloween is cool!
Mom and Dad were confused.
Who is Halloween?
When will he get here?
Halloween is not a person!
Halloween is a holiday!
You wear costumes!
And go to people's houses!
And get tasty treats!
And carve pumpkins!

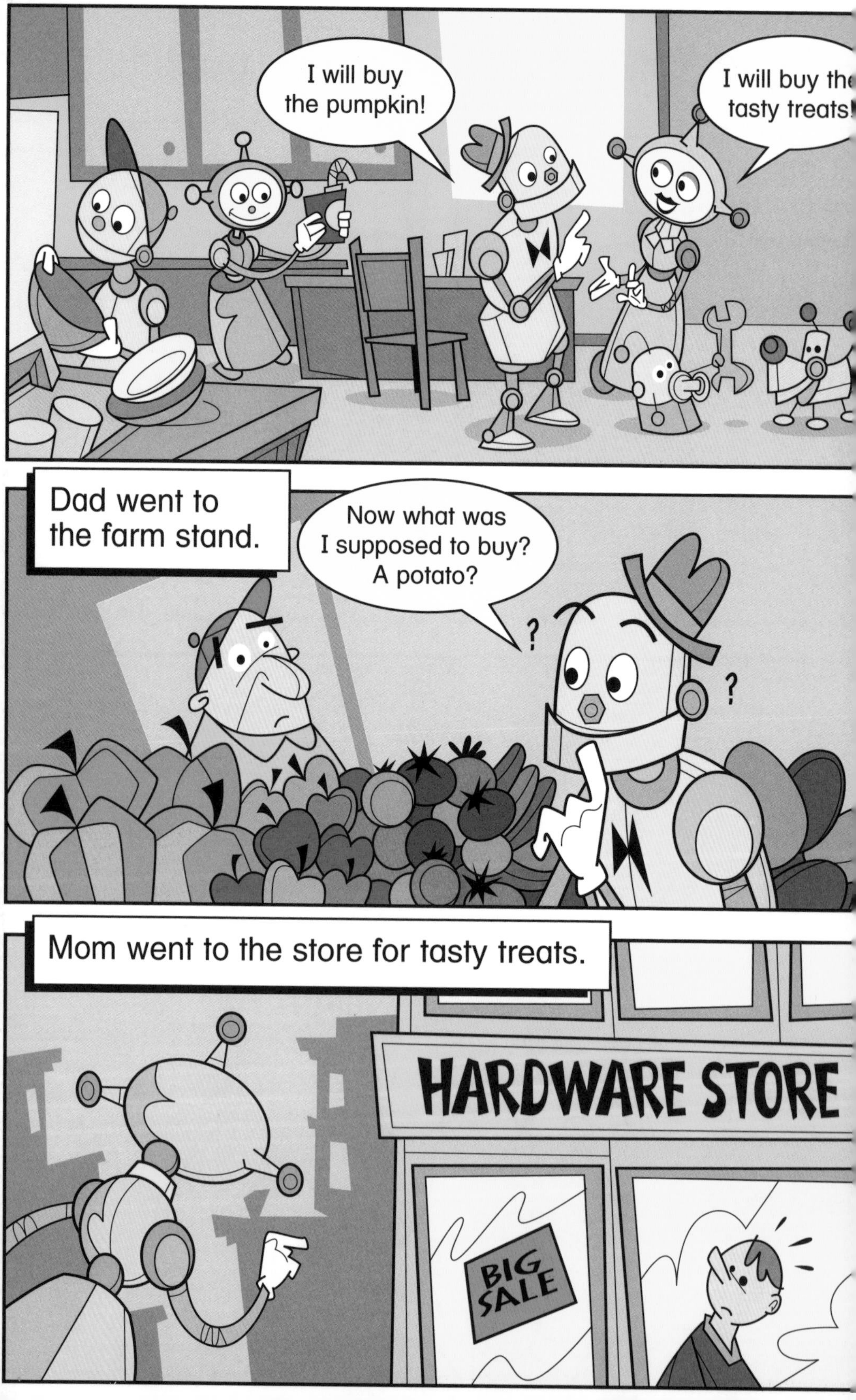
I will buy the pumpkin!
I will buy th tasty treats!
Dad went to the farm stand.
Now what was I supposed to buy? A potato?
?
?
Mom went to the store for tasty treats.
HARDWARE STORE
BIG SALE

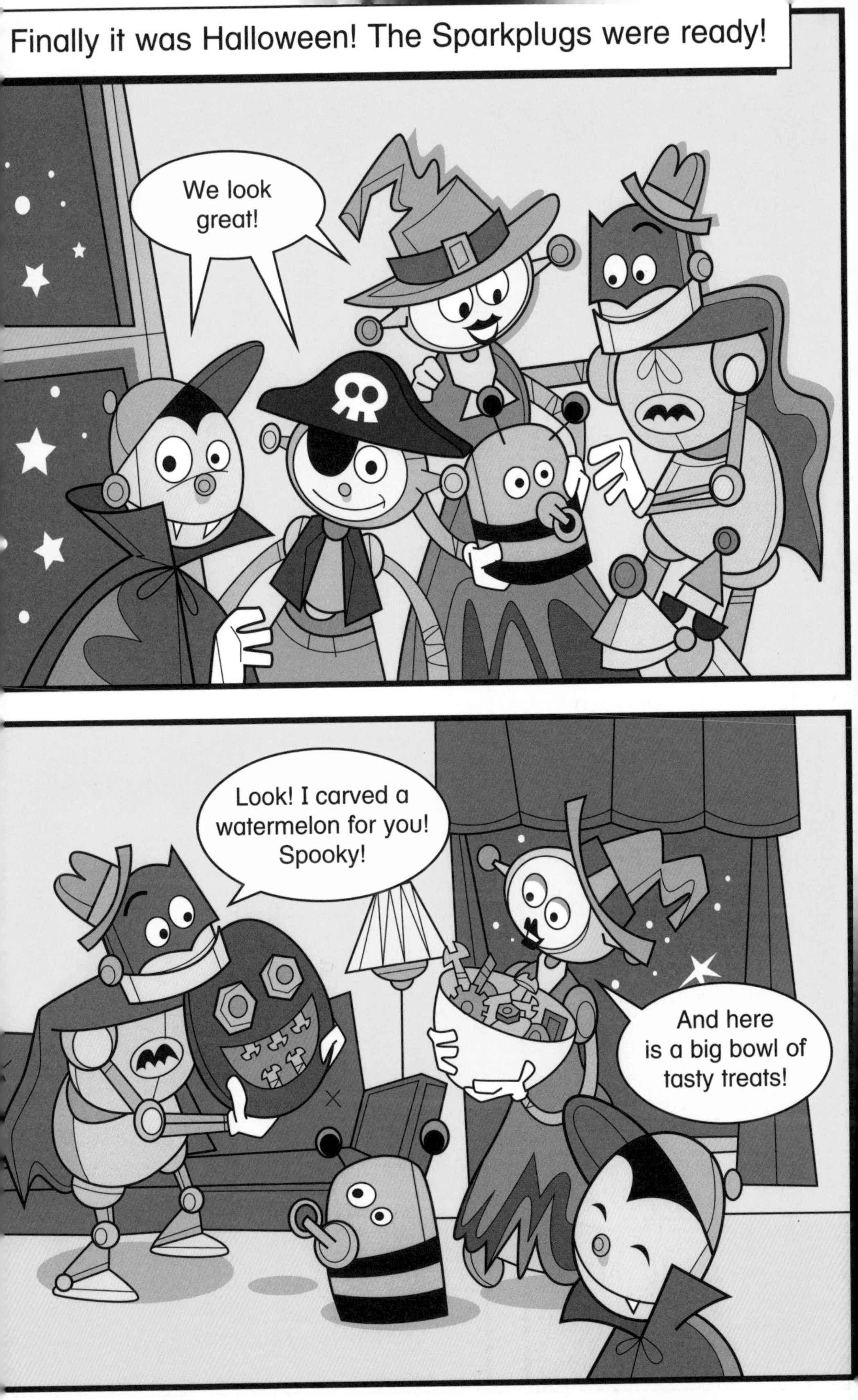
Finally it was Halloween! The Sparkplugs were ready!
We look great!
Look! I carved a watermelon for you! Spooky!
And here is a big bowl of tasty treats!

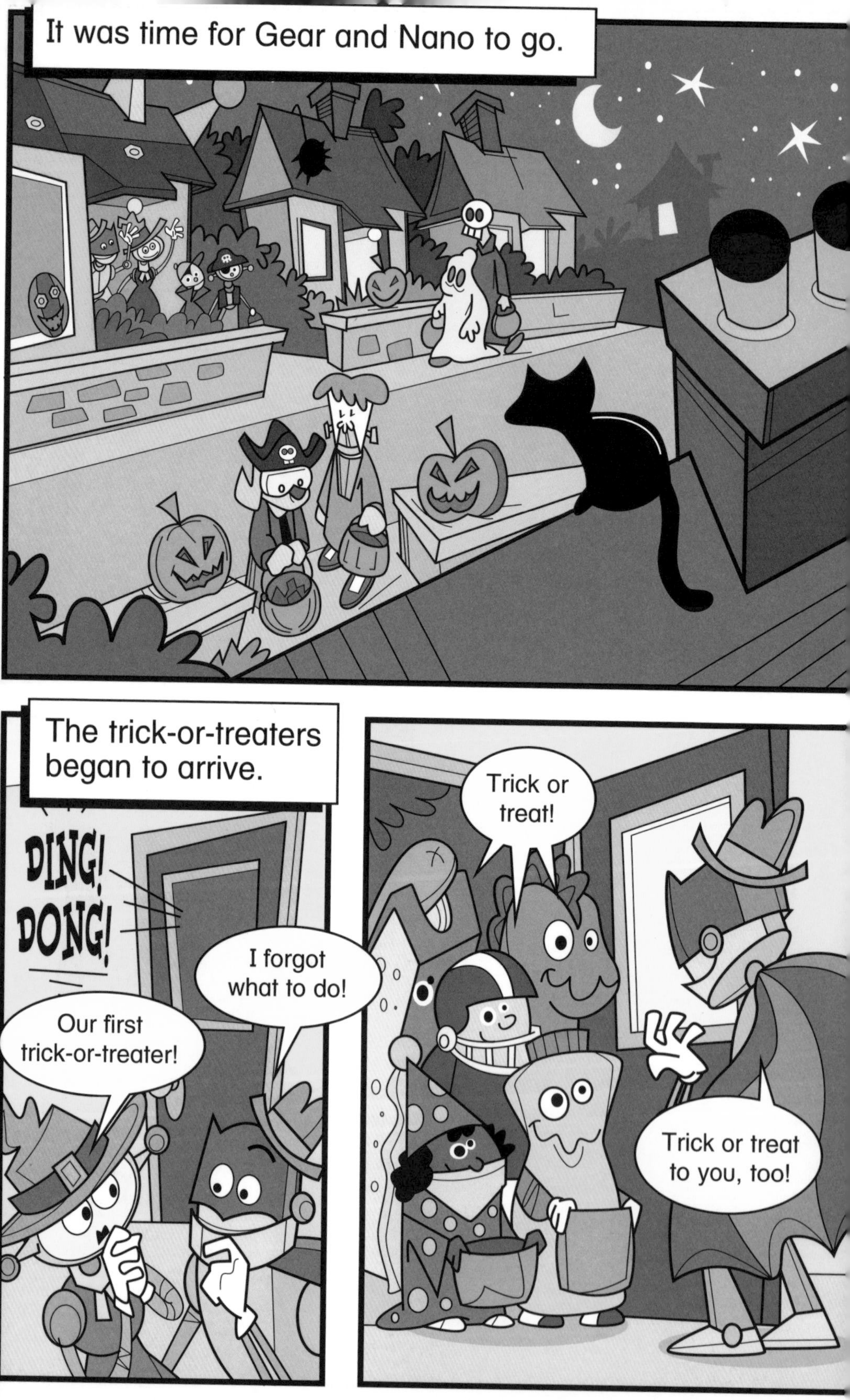
It was time for Gear and Nano to go.
The trick-or-treaters began to arrive.
DING! DONG!
I forgot what to do!
Our first trick-or-treater!
Trick or treat!
Trick or treat to you, too!

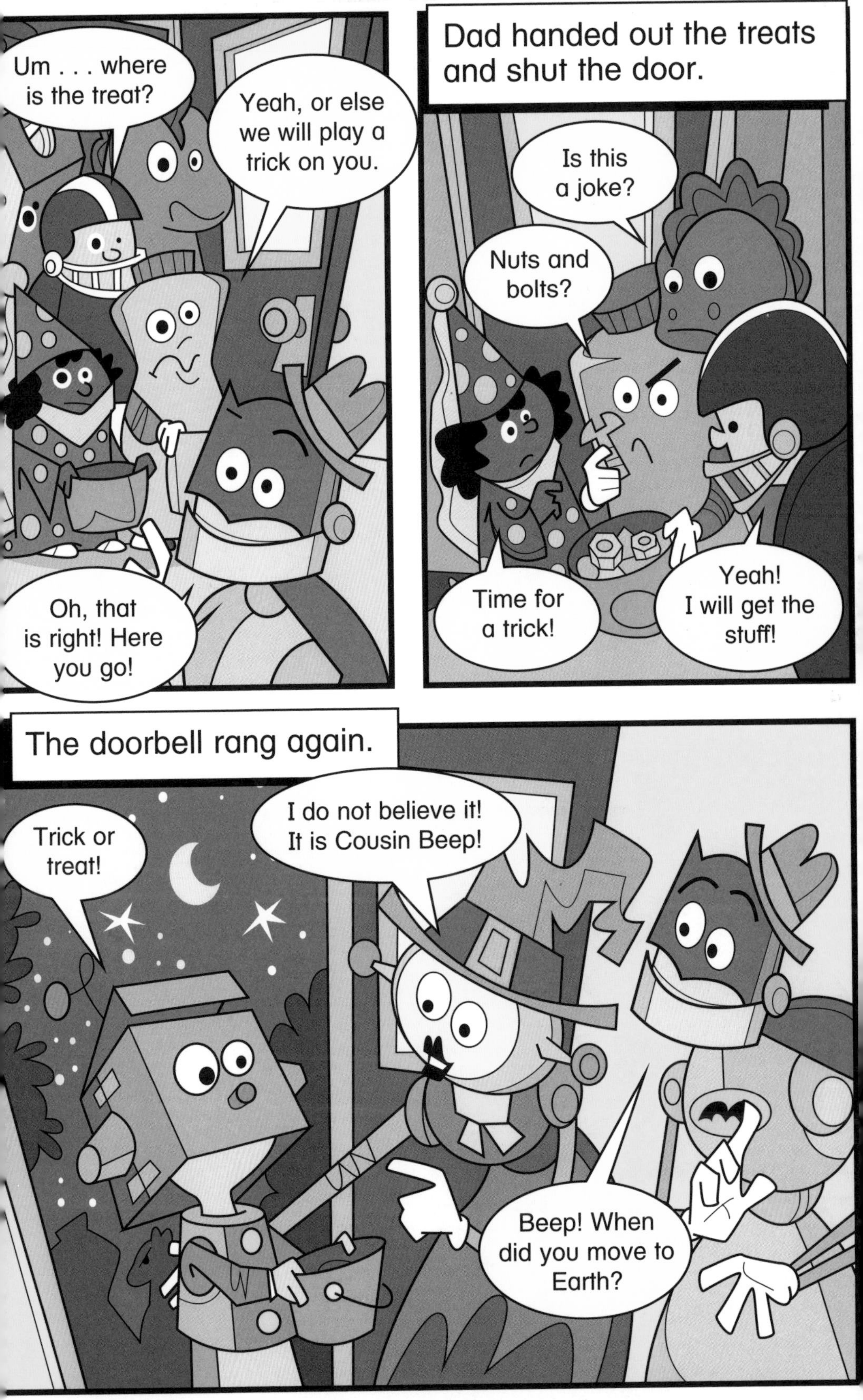
Um . . . where is the treat?
Yeah, or else we will play a trick on you.
Oh, that is right! Here you go!
Dad handed out the treats and shut the door.
Is this a joke?
Nuts and bolts?
Time for a trick!
Yeah! I will get the stuff!
The doorbell rang again.
Trick or treat!
I do not believe it! It is Cousin Beep!
Beep! When did you move to Earth?

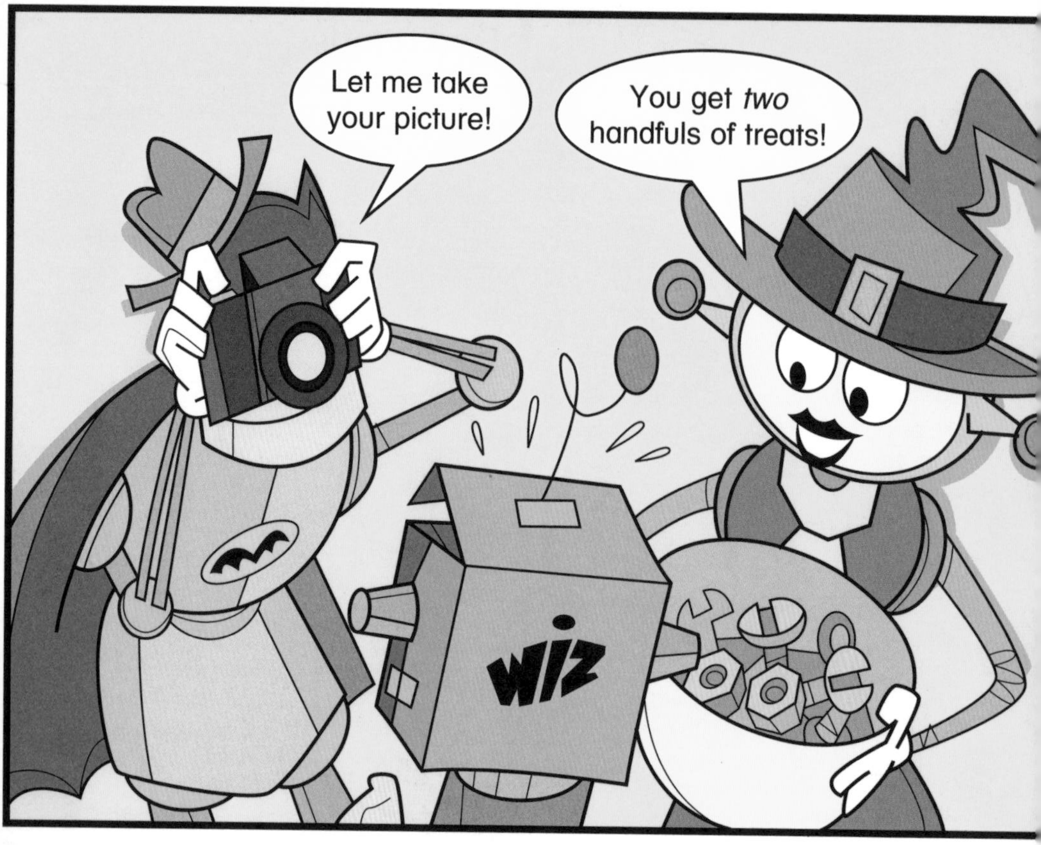
Let me take your picture!
You get *two* handfuls of treats!
WIZ

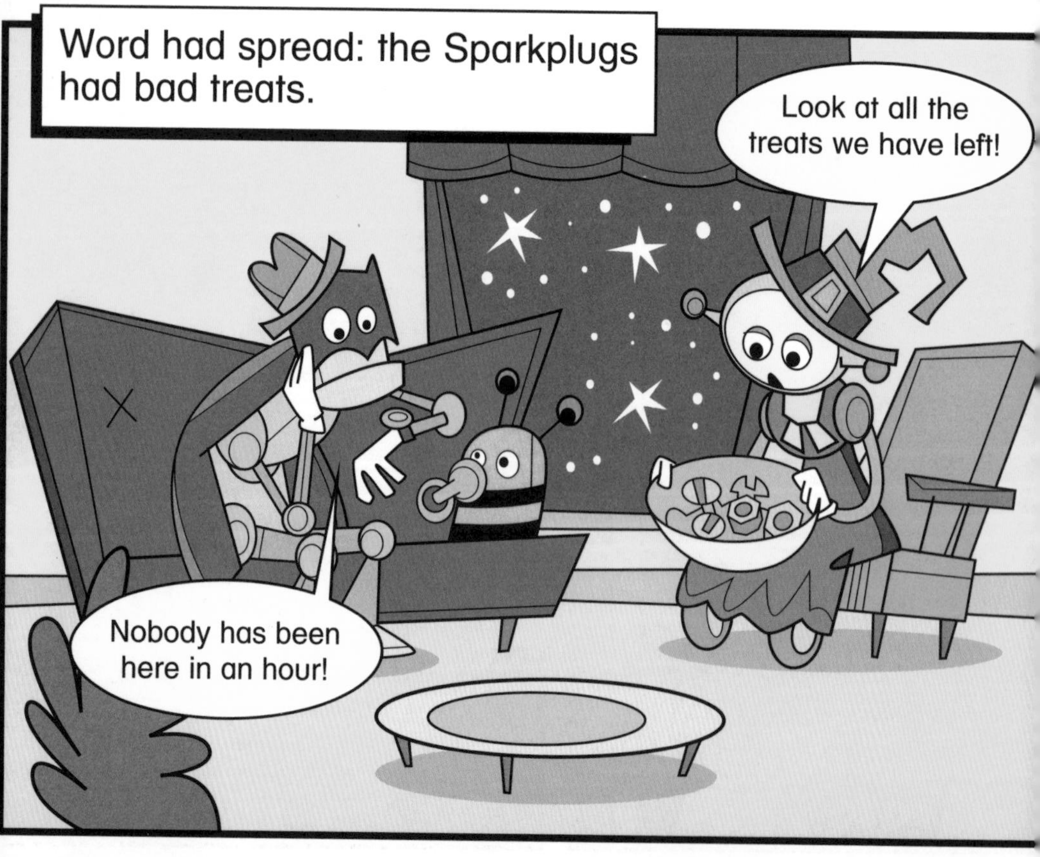
Word had spread: the Sparkplugs had bad treats.
Look at all the treats we have left!
Nobody has been here in an hour!

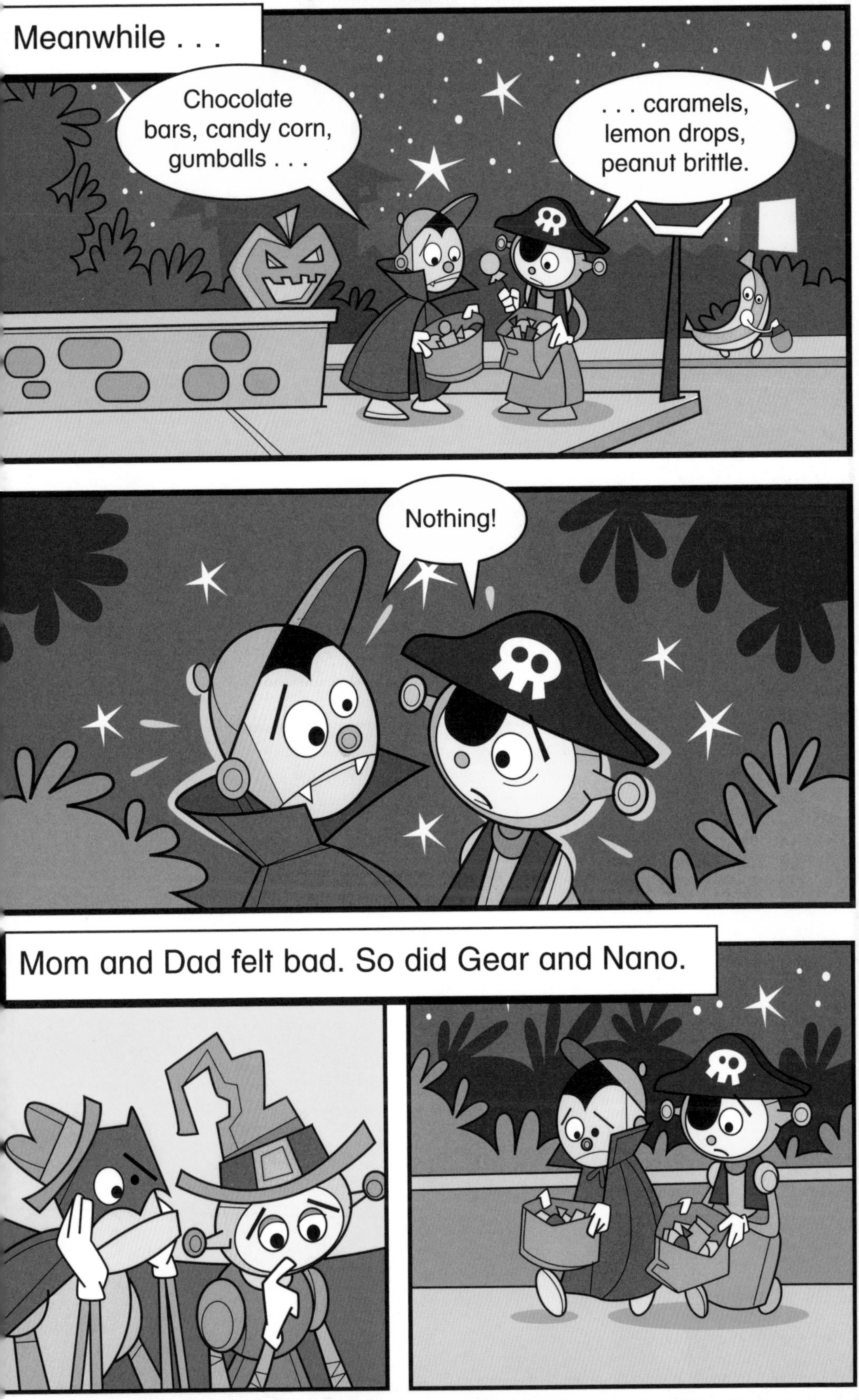
Meanwhile . . .
Chocolate bars, candy corn, gumballs . . .
. . . caramels, lemon drops, peanut brittle.
Nothing!
Mom and Dad felt bad. So did Gear and Nano.

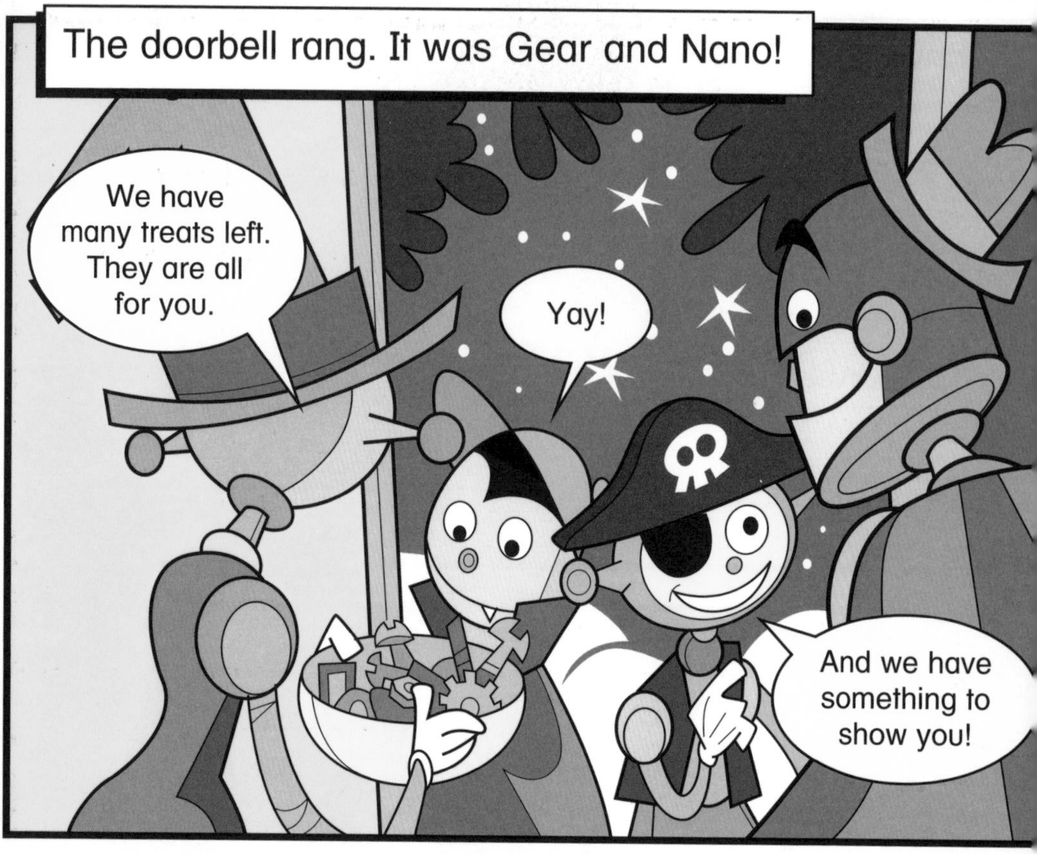
The doorbell rang. It was Gear and Nano!
We have many treats left. They are all for you.
Yay!
And we have something to show you!

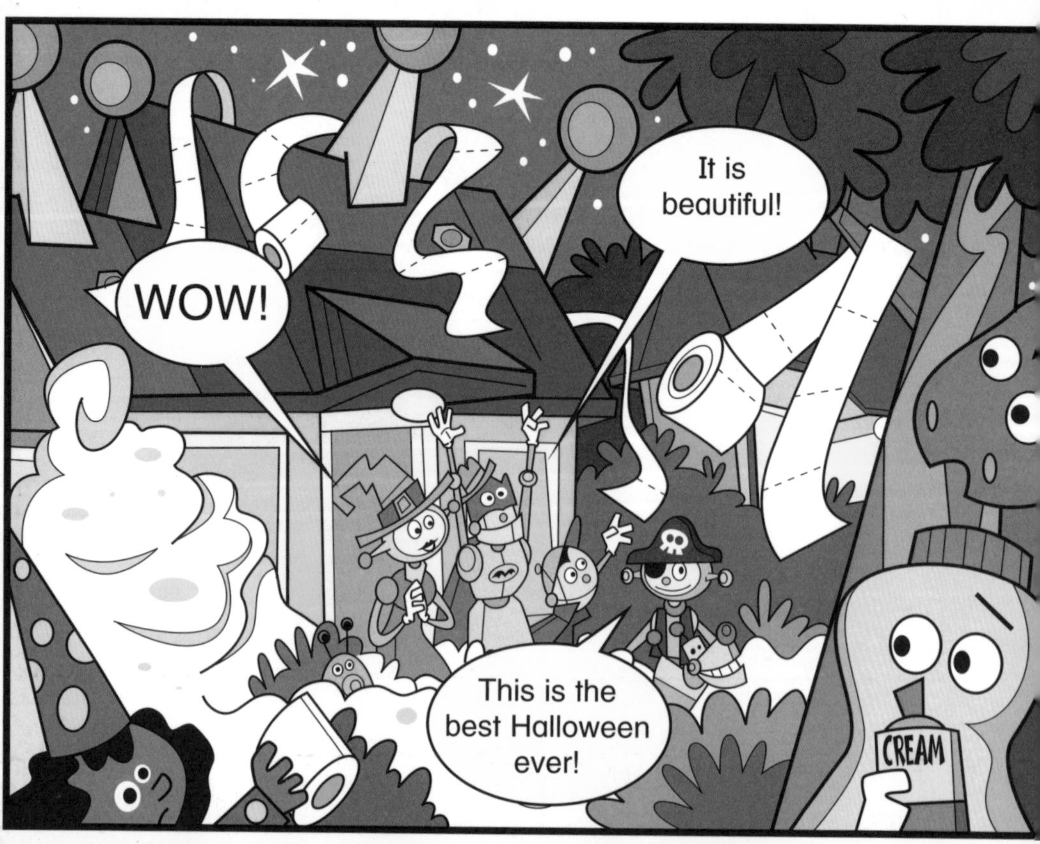
WOW!
It is beautiful!
This is the best Halloween ever!
CREAM